Anonymous

Supplemental Catalogue of Canadian Apparatus

Anonymous

Supplemental Catalogue of Canadian Apparatus

Reprint of the original, first published in 1859.

1st Edition 2022 | ISBN: 978-3-37512-214-0

Verlag (Publisher): Salzwasser Verlag GmbH, Zeilweg 44, 60439 Frankfurt, Deutschland
Vertretungsberechtigt (Authorized to represent): E. Roepke, Zeilweg 44, 60439 Frankfurt, Deutschland
Druck (Print): Books on Demand GmbH, In de Tarpen 42, 22848 Norderstedt, Deutschland

SUPPLEMENTAL CATALOGUE

OF

CANADIAN APPARATUS,

Globes, Maps, and School Requisites,

FOR

SALE TO PUBLIC SCHOOLS

AT THE

Upper Canada Educational Depository.

TORONTO:

Printed for the Department of Public Instruction for Upper Canada,

BY LOVELL AND GIBSON,

1859.

TERMS—STRICTLY CASH.

In transmitting an order for any of the articles for sale at the Depository, care must be taken to accompany it with a remittance, and also to give directions as to the parties to whom the parcel should be sent. The sole object of this Department is to provide facilities for supplying the Public Schools of Upper Canada with approved Books, Maps, and Apparatus, at cost. When the article ordered is not in stock, the nearest selection to it is made, subject, however, to the approval of the Trustees, &c. Nearly all the Apparatus sent out is of Canadian manufacture.

Just Published,

RAISED MAPS (IN COMPOSITION PLASTER)

OF

ANCIENT AND MODERN GREECE AND ITALY.

Price of each Map, coloured, mounted, and packed, $15.

FREFATORY NOTE.

It is gratifying to state, that the chief part of the Apparatus which is is now supplied to the public schools of Upper Canada, by the Educational Department, has been manufactured in Toronto, under the direction of the Department.

This branch of home industry has been gradually introduced and carefully fostered, and renders this reference to it no less a pleasure to the Head of the Department than a just tribute to the energetic and enterprising zeal of the persons who are engaged in its prosecution.* It is highly creditable to these parties to state, that their work is generally not only equal in point of excellence to the English and American makers, but, in many cases, it is quite superior, and, at the same time, cheaper. To the attainment of this most desirable object, has the attention of the Department been sedulously directed; while it has also sought to suggest such improvements and alterations as appeared desirable and practicable; and where none were necessary, it was deemed by the Department essential that in point of finish and adaptation to the objects in view, the article of Canadian manufacture should compare favorably with its English or American prototype.

Specimens of the articles manufactured in Toronto, have been exhibited at the several Provincial Fairs, and excited a good deal of attention and commendation. The Apparatus manufactured include not only school desks and seats, but maps, map-cases, and rotary stands; brass orreries, tellurians, globes, geometrical figures, and diagrams; mechanical powers, levers, and various articles of brass work, illustrative of the different branches of natural philosophy. A detailed list of these articles, together with a number of valuable additions to the Depository Catalogue, will be found in the following pages.

---

* Messrs. Jacques & Hay, (Manufacturers of Map-Stands, Cases, Globes, Geometrical Forms, Mechanical Powers, &c.); Mr. Charles Potter, (Brass-work, Orreries, &c.); Messrs. Maclear & Co., (Lithographers); Mr. John Carter, (Map Mounter, &c.)

In addition to the apparatus, arrangements have been made, not only to have the maps mounted in Canada, (which has been done for years), but also to have the various maps and globe covers engraved and lithographed in this country. This arrangement has been highly successful.

As it is the object of the Department to bring within the reach of private parties excellent and beautiful articles of school apparatus, as well as provide them for the public schools, it has been suggested to the manufacturers of them,* to not merely execute the orders of the Department, but to provide and keep a supply on hand, (as the Department can only supply municipal and school authorities with school requisites), for sale to all who may desire them, that gentlemen may thus be able to procure these important and pleasing aids to instruction for their own families; and we are sure they will not be the less sought for and the less valued, when it is considered that they are the productions of Canadian skill and enterprise.

The plan of the Department of Public Instruction, has been to import nothing that can be produced at home ; to furnish patterns, and to suggest and offer encouragement to attempts for the manufacture at home of all the material appliances of school instruction. The experiment was commenced with the printing of school books and the manufacture of school furniture ; it has proved completely successful ; and every subsequent experiment has been equally decisive on the side of Canadian skill and industry. Thus in everything appertaining to our schools, from the training of the teacher and the architecture and furnishing of the school-house, to the smallest article of school apparatus, our system is becoming more completely Canadian, and proportionably efficient.

---

* *i.e.* those named in the note on page iii.

CONTENTS.

	PAGE
	iii
Prefatory Note	vii
Departmental Notices	9
Map Stands and Cases	13
Other Important Maps, Charts, and Diagrams	14
Johnston's Modern Globes	17
Canadian School Apparatus	22
Natural Philosophy	25
Hydrostatics and Hydraulics	26
Steam	26
Pneumatics	30
Electricity	32
Magnetism and Electro-Magnetism	39
Natural History	39
Heat	40
Chemistry	41
Drawing and Mathematical Instruments	42
Zoology	42
Physiology and Zoology	44
Botany	44
Text Books authorized for use in the Grammar Schools	44
1. Latin	45
2. Greek	45
Classical Dictionaries, &c.	46
3. French	46
4. English	47
5. Mathematics	47
6. Geography and History	48
7. Physical Science	48
8. Miscellaneous	49
Drawing Books, Materials, and Models	52
Writing	53
Maps, Charts, and Diagrams of Physical Geography	54
Geological Maps, Diagrams, and Cabinets	54

DEPARTMENTAL NOTICES.

PUBLIC SCHOOL LIBRARIES.

" Township and County Libraries are becoming the crown and glory of the Institutions of the Province."—Lord Elgin at the Upper Canada Provincial Exhibition, September, 1854.

The Chief Superintendent of Education is prepared to apportion *one hundred per cent.* upon all sums which shall be raised from local sources by Municipal Councils and School Corporations, for the establishment or increase of Public Libraries in Upper Canada, under the regulations provided according to law. Prison Libraries, and Teachers' County Association Libraries, may, under these regulations, be established by County Councils, as branch libraries.

SCHOOL MAPS AND APPARATUS.

The Chief Superintendent will add one hundred per cent. to any sum or sums, not less than five dollars, transmitted to the Department by Municipal and School Corporations on behalf of Grammar and Common Schools; and forward Maps, Apparatus, Charts, and Diagrams to the value of the amount thus augmented, upon receiving a list of the articles required. In all cases it will be necessary for any person, acting on behalf of the Municipality or Trustees, to enclose or present a written authority to do so, verified by the corporate seal of the Corporation. A selection of articles to be sent can always be made by the Department, when so desired.

PRIZES IN SCHOOLS.

The Chief Superintendent will grant one hundred per cent. upon all sums not less than five dollars transmitted to him by Municipalities or Boards of School Trustees for the purchase of books or reward cards for prizes in Grammar and Common Schools. Catalogues and Forms forwarded upon application.

SCHOOL MAPS AND APPARATUS.

(CANADIAN MANUFACTURE.)

I. MAP STANDS AND CASES.

The following addition to the last edition of the *Descriptive Catalogue*, contains illustrations of various kinds of School Apparatus which have been recently manufactured in Toronto, under the direction of the Educational Department. They are supplied to the Schools at the prices annexed, and upon the terms stated in the Departmental Notice relating

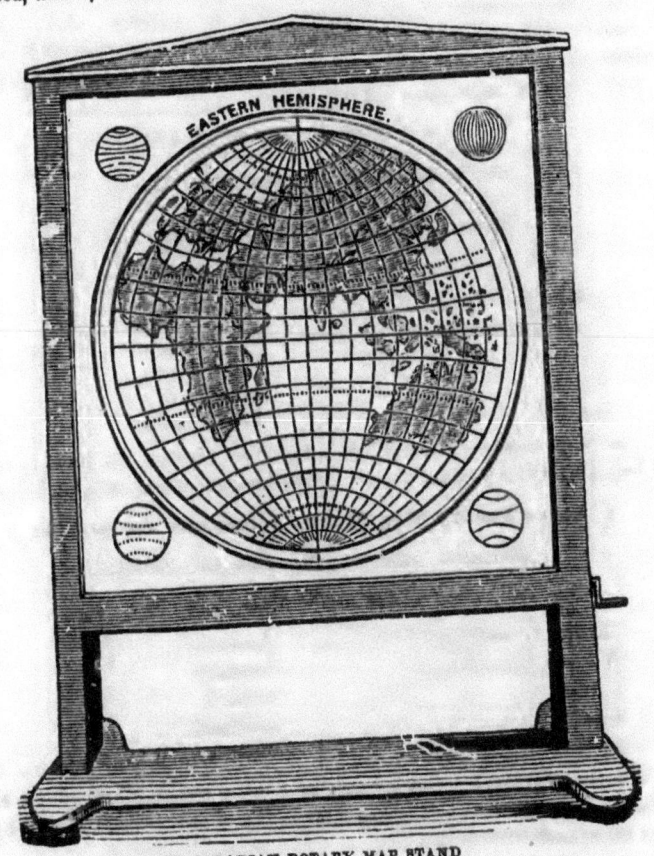

CANADIAN ROTARY MAP STAND

to Maps and Apparatus. (See page iv.) This pamphlet also contains all the late additions of other articles which have been added to the Depository list. Explanatory and Descriptive Notes of the Apparatus have been added where it was thought desirable.

1. Canadian Rotary Map Stand—National Series.—No I.

The Stand is mounted on castors, and contains Ten Colored Maps on a continuous web of cloth, which revolves vertically, over rollers, by turning the handle at the side, so that the maps are exhibited in rotation. An outside cover of oak paper contains the following List of the Maps:

Canada (and Text-Book.)	Pacific Ocean.
United States.	Scripture World.
Europe.	Orbis Veteribus Notus.
Asia.	Græcia Antiqua.
Australia.	Italia Antiqua.

The Maps measure 5 feet 6 inches by 4 feet 4 inches. The Stand is 6 feet 10 inches high by 6 feet broad, with Blackboard behind for arithmetic or diagrams. It can be taken to pieces, packed, and sent with safety to any part of the country. Price $88.00.

The price of separate maps are $3 and $3.50.

2. National Series.—No. II.

(This is mounted in the same style as No. I.)

List of the Maps.

Eastern Hemisphere.	Ireland,
Western Hemisphere.	Scotland.
America.	Palestine.
Africa.	Asia Minor.
England.	Terra Sancta.

The Maps measure 5 feet 6 inches by 4 feet 4 inches, the stand is 8 feet 4 inches by 4 feet 8 inches broad. Price $38, or for the two stands $75.

3. Large Rotary Map Stand—Johnstons' Series.—No. I.

(Mounted same as the National Series.)

List of the Maps.

Eastern Hemisphere.	America.
Western Hemisphere.	England.
Europe.	Ireland,
Asia.	Scotland.
Africa.	Canada, (and Text Book.)

The Maps measure 4 feet 2 inches by 3 feet 6 inches, the stand is 6 feet 9 inches high by 4 feet 8 inches broad. Price $34. Single maps $2.38 and $2.88 each.

4. Large Rotary Map Stand—Johnstons' Series.—No. II:

(Same as the preceding.)

List of the Maps.

France.
Spain.
Central Europe.
Italy.
India.

Orbis Veteribus Notus.
Orbis Romanus.
Italia Antiqua.
Græcia Antiqua.
Canaan and Palestine.

The Maps measure 4 feet 2 inches by 3 feet 6 inches, the stand is 6 feet 9 inches high by 4 feet 8 inches broad. Price $34, or for the two stands $67.

5. Small Rotary Map Stand—Johnstons' Series.—No. I.

List of the Maps.

Eastern Hemisphere.
Western Hemisphere.
Europe.
Asia.
Africa.

America.
England.
Ireland.
Scotland.
Canaan and Palestine.

The Maps measure 2 feet 9 inches by 2 feet 3 inches, the stand is 6 feet high by 3 feet 2 inches broad. Price $25.

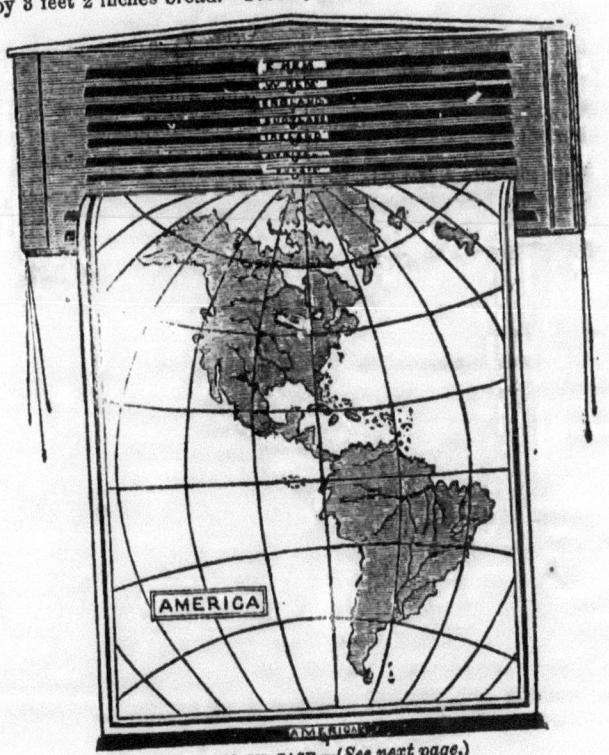

MAPS IN CASE.—(*See next page.*)

6. Set of Large Maps in Case—Johnstons' Series.—No. I.

The Case for hanging on a Wall contains 10 Coloured Maps on Cloth and Rollers, and is so constructed that any Map can be drawn down as required, and pulled up again by the cords at the side.

List of the Maps.

Eastern Hemisphere.	America.
Western Hemisphere.	England.
Europe.	Scotland.
Asia.	Ireland.
Africa.	Canada, (and Text Book.

The Maps measure 4 feet 2 inches by 3 feet 6 inches. The case is 4 feet 8 inches long by 1 foot 9 inches high; and as it is only 4 inches thick, it projects very little from the wall. It can be packed and sent with safety to any part of the country. Price $24.

7. Set of Large Maps in Case—Johnstons' Series.—No. II.

(Mounted same as Case No. I.)

List of the Maps.

France.	Orbis Veteribus Notus.
Spain.	Orbis Romanus.
Central Europe.	Italia Antiqua.
Italy.	Græcia Antiqua.
India.	Canaan and Palestine.

The Maps measure 4 feet 2 inches by 3 feet 6 inches. The case is 4 feet 8 inches long by 1 foot 9 inches high. Price $24.

8. Set of Small Maps in Case—Johnstons' Series.—No. I.

List of the Maps.

Eastern Hemisphere.	America.
Western Hemisphere.	England.
Europe.	Ireland.
Asia.	Scotland.
Africa.	Palestine.

Size of the Maps 33 by 27 inches. Size of the case 3 feet 3 inches by 1 foot 6 inches. Price $16. Singly $1.38.

II. OTHER ELABORATE AND IMPORTANT MAPS, CHARTS AND DIAGRAMS.

9. Johnstons' General Map of Europe, shewing the present Political Divisions of Europe, on a scale 76 miles to an inch; it also contains the names of battles and sieges which occurred during the beginning of the present century; the Sea tracks, distances of important ports, lines of railway, &c., and, besides, show the more important physical features. Size, 4 feet 2 inches by 3 feet 5 inches. Price, mounted and varnished, $8.

10. Johnstons' Commercial Chart of the World, on Mercator's Projection; with Captains M'Clure and Belcher's discoveries to 1853.— Shewing the relative importance of the princip Towns, the Railways of the Continent, Canals, and Roads; the extent of the *Zollverein,* or German Commercial Union, with a list of its Exports, Imports, &c

Enlarged Maps of the principal Colonies, and Plans of important Seaports—British Colonies—Table of Distances—Overland Route to India— Time Table—Currents of the Ocean—Steam Packet Routes—Soundings —Ice—Bearings and Distances—Fucus Bank—Naval Engagements, &c. Size—6 feet by 4 feet 8 inches. Price $11.

10. Johnston's Geological Map of Europe, exhibiting the different systems of Rocks, according to the latest researches, and from unedited materials. Scale $\frac{1}{4.500.00}$ of nature, 76 miles to 1 inch. Size of Map 4 feet 2 inches by 3 feet 5 inches. Price, mounted and varnished, $15.

11. Johnston's General Map of the United States and British North America, constructed from the most recent documents, procured from the different Departments of Government, and valuable unpublished materials. Scale $\frac{1}{3.450.00}$ of nature, or 54½ miles to an inch. Size 6 feet by 4 feet 8 inches. Price $10.

12. Chambers' Map of the World, containing separate Maps of Australia, New Zealand, and Van Diemen's Land; also, illustrations of the annual revolution of the Earth round the Sun, the Theory of the Seasons, Tides, Phases of the Moon, &c., together with a comparative view of the principal Mountains and Rivers in the World. Size, 5 feet 4 inches by 4 feet 5 inches. Price $4.

13. Day & Son's Orthographic Projection of the World.—By Richard Abbatt, F.R.A.S. The Perspective View of the Earth, or Visible Hemisphere, is three feet in diameter, and exhibits the Continental Divisions, Geographical Features, the Seas, Islands, Chief Cities and Towns, from China to the Andes, and from Cape Town to the Aleutian Islands. The Eye, or Point of Sight, is situated vertically over Lat. 45° N., and in the Plane of the Meridian of London, and embraces in their true and natural positions Countries and Cities containing upwards of 750,000,000 of Inhabitants. Size, 3 feet 4 inches by 3 feet 8 inches. Price, coloured, varnished and mounted, with Hand Book to accompany it, $6.

14. Day & Son's World of the Antipodes,—By Richard Abbatt, F.R.A.S. In this View the Point of Sight is situated over Lat. 45° S., Long. 180°, and embraces the opposite Hemisphere of the Earth, having the same boundary for the Horizon as the other Map. The position of the East-India Islands, Australia, New Zealand, the Groups of Islands studded over the Pacific Ocean, the Western portion of South America, and the Ocean Routes by Cape Horn and the Cape of Good Hope, are here rendered perfectly intelligible. Both Maps are embellished with natural and artificial features. Size, 3 feet 6 inches by 3 feet 8 inches. Price, colored, varnished and mounted, $6.

15. Day & Son's American Sub-Marine Chart, shewing the Telegraphic Communication about to be established between Newfoundland and Ireland; the track of Steamers between Europe and America; and the Ice-Fields in the North Atlantic Ocean. To which is added a section of the bottom of the Atlantic, from Valentia Bay, Ireland, to St. John's, Newfoundland, obtained by Soundings taken by the United States Steamer Arctic. Also, sections, full size, of the Electric Cables to be submerged., Size, 3 feet by 2 feet. Price, coloured, mounted and varnished, $1.10.

16. Smith's Large Outline Map of the World on Mercator's Projection.—Size 8 feet 6 inches wide, 5 feet 8 inches deep. This Map shows, in bold outline, a skeleton representation of the World, including Mountain Ranges, Rivers, Boundaries of Countries, and positions of the principal Towns, compiled at the suggestion of many Scientific Gentlemen as a Map much wanted for the illustration of Lectures on Physical Geography. Price on rollers, $4.50.

III. JOHNSTON'S MODERN GLOBES,*

With the most recent Discoveries.

17. Eighteen inch Globes, high Mahogany Stands, with Compass and Quadrant, per pair, like Fig. 1 (*next page*) $90 00
18. do   do   do   singly...... 46 00
19. Twelve inch Globes, high Mahogany Stands, with Compass and Quadrants, per pair, like Fig. 1...................... 40 00
20. do   do   do   singly...... 21 00

* Now being constructed in Toronto.

FIG. I.   FIG. II.

21. Thirty inch Terrestrial Globe, with Black Stand and Quadrant, like Fig. 2, with barrel for packing ditto............. $65 00
22. Eighteen inch Globes, low Black Stands and Quad., per pair, like Fig. 2.. 60 00
23.   do   do   do   singly.. .. 31 00
24. Eighteen inch Globes, low Mahogany Stands and Quadrant, per pair, like Fig. 2....................................... 70 00
25.   do   do   do   singly...... 36 00
26. Twelve inch Globes, low Black Stands and Quadr, per pair, like Fig. 2.. 27 00
27.   do   do   do   singly...... 14 00
28. Six inch Terrestrial Globe, Black Walnut Stand............ 1 50
    Do. on Bronzed Stand, with brass semi-frame meridian . 2 00

———

Educational Department Globes, compiled from the most recent authorities, and constructed in Toronto under its supervision and direction.   ———

29. **The Celestial Improved Sphere,** with 6 inch central Globe, shews the great circles of the heavens, the meridians, equator and ecliptic. The ecliptic is divided into the twelve signs of the zodiac, and marked with the days of the year. The axis of the earth may be inclined at any desired angle.

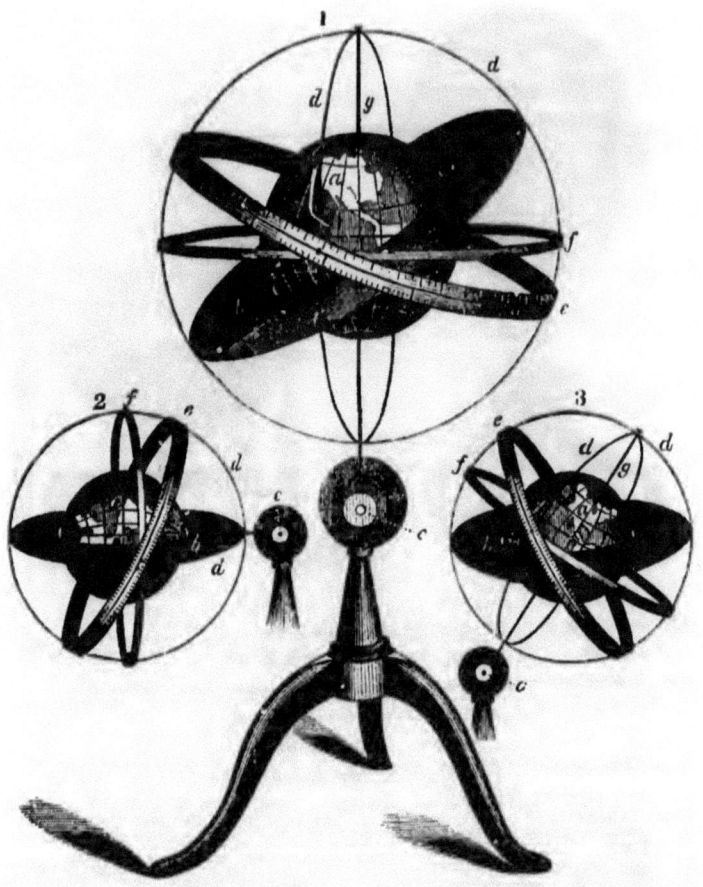

CELESTIAL IMPROVED SPHERE.

A horizon plane is attached by which the real horizon of any place on the globe may be shewn, also the comparative lengths of day and night on any part of the earth, and at any season, the rising and setting of the sun, together with the sun's place in the ecliptic on any day in the year. Price $6.

———

30. **Tide Dial,** 15 inches diameter, which, by turning a crank, illustrates the Daily Changes in the Tides, the Diurnal Motion of the Earth, Causes of Eclipses, and shows the Earth's Umbra and Penumbra; with Gilt Sun, on stand. Price $6.50.

CANADIAN SCHOOL APPARATUS.

31. The Orrery, 3 feet in diameter, represents the proportional size and relative position of the Planets composing the Solar System, except the asteroids, and shows their annual revolutions. A correct idea of the Solar System is seldom received, except by such aid. With it, we see the Planets and their Moons circling round their common centre, each in its separate orbit, and occupying its own place in the ecliptic—and system is developed from the seeming chaos of the stars. Price $10.

ORRERY.

TELLURIAN, &C.

32. The Tellurian is designed to illustrate the various phenomena resulting from the relations of the Sun, Moon and Earth to each other; the succession of day and night, the change of the seasons, the change of the Sun's declination, the different lengths of day and night, the changes of the moon, the harvest moon, the procession of the equinoxes, the differences of a solar and sidereal year, &c. The Moon revolves around the Earth, and both together around the Sun, while Sun, Earth and Moon revolve around a common centre of gravity. Price $6.

33. The Lunarian, for illustrating the phases of the Moon and centre of gravity. Price $1.

SIX INCH GLOBE.—(FIG. 1.)   (FIG. 2.)

34. A 6 inch **Terrestrial Globe**, with the latest discoveries, strongly made of firm material, and so mounted on a single pedestal that it can be

readily removed and suspended by a cord, and thus be displayed convenient-
ly for familiar illustrations to a class. It is of a convenient size for common
use in the school-room, as it can be easily held in the hand, or passed round
the class and yet answers all the main ends of the larger sized globes.
Price, on walnut Pedestal (Fig. 1), $1.50; on bronzed Stand, with brass
Semi-frame Meridian (Fig. 2), $2.

35. A 3 inch **Hemisphere Globe,** supplies an illustration, which any
child can understand, of the reason of the curved lines on a map, and
shews how the flat surface is a proper representation of a globe. It is the

THREE INCH HEMISPHERE GLOBE.

result of a suggestion from a practical teacher. Two hemispheres are
united by a hinge, and when closed a neat little globe is presented; when
opened, two maps are seen, showing the continents, as if through transparent hemispheres. Price, 75 cts.

36. A set of Geometrical Solids.—These will give pupils definite
ideas of the shape of the solids. far better than pages of description, and

CUBES.

much more clearly than any drawings can. We know nothing better. For explaining the Rules for Mensuration or Solid Measurement, they afford the only proper means. Price, $1 25 to $1 75.

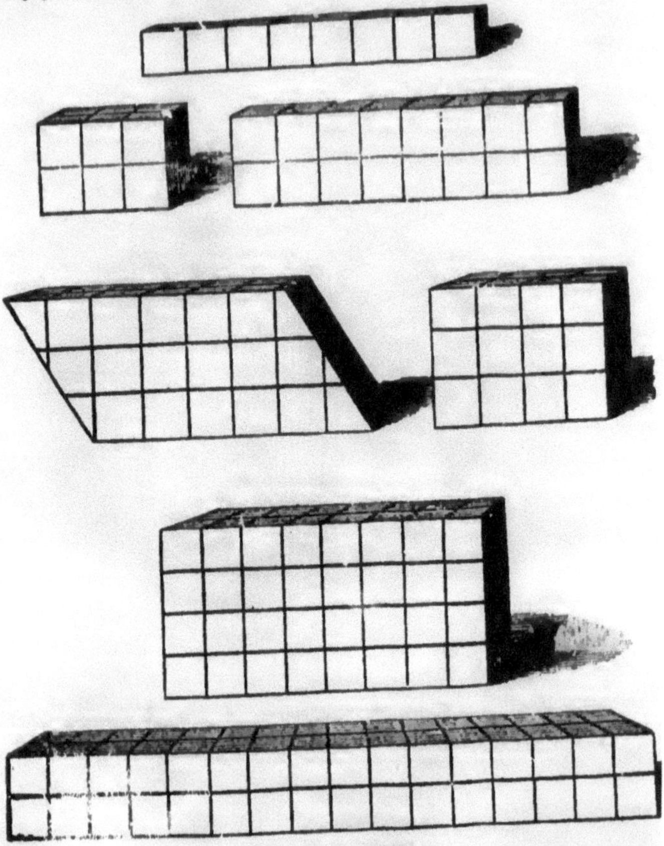

PARALLELOPIPEDS.

OBLATE SPHEROID.   SPHERE.   PROLATE SPHEROI

HEXAGONAL PRISM.   PRISM.   TRIANGULAR PRISM.   CYLINDER.

PYRAMID AND FRUSTUM.   CONE AND FRUSTUM.

37. The **Numeral Frame** was designed for Primary Schools, but has proved of nearly equal service in intermediate and Grammar Schools; wherever young pupils require illustrations to enable them fully to comprehend operations with abstract mathematical quantities, this frame furnishes the readiest mode of giving the desired instruction. Price 75 cts

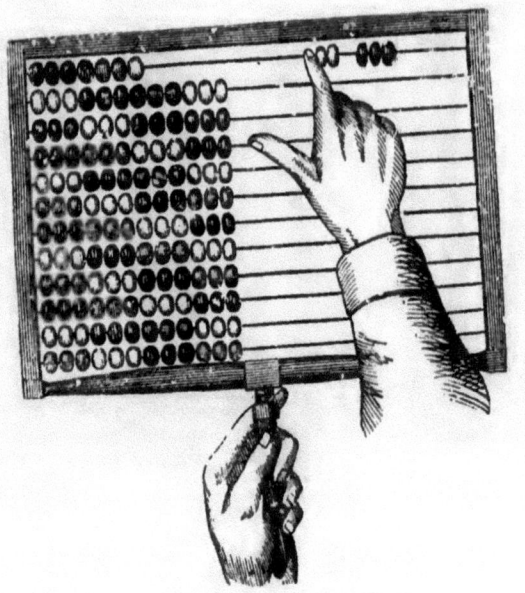

THE NUMERAL FRAME.

38. Teachers' Guide, a Manual to accompany the Apparatus, revised by the Educational Department, U. C. Price 50 cts.

39. Price for the entire set, packed in a neat box, containing the following articles, $20:

Viz.:

(1) Brass Mounted Orrery.
(2) Brass Mounted Tellurian.
(3) Lunarian.
(4) Six Inch Globe.

(5) Three Inch Hemisphere Globe.
(6) Set of Forms and Solids.
(7) Numeral Frame.
(8) Teacher's Guide.

NATURAL PHILOSOPHY.

MECHANICS.

The Mechanical Powers are certain agents, applied to machinery constructed in accordance with the laws of nature, to enable man to over come resistance in raising weights, moving bodies, &c.; they consist of th Lever, the Wheel and Axle, the Pulley, the Inclined Plane, the Wedge an the Screw, although by these contrivances man is enabled to perform an work in proportion to the speed of power he can command, yet, the adva tage gained is simply an advantage of pressure, not of work; for what gained in pressure is lost in speed; whenever power is gained sometni is lost to counter-balance it, practical men express this law by saying " *wh* *you gain in power you lose in speed."* . If a man can lift a hundred pounds with his hands alone, he may be able to lift one thousand pounds by the aid of a lever, but it will take him ten times as long to lift it through the same space.

The real advantage to be derived from the use of these models, is not only a practical knowledge of the appliances of the *simple* machines, but, to impress upon the mind of the pupil that one man, by working proportionably

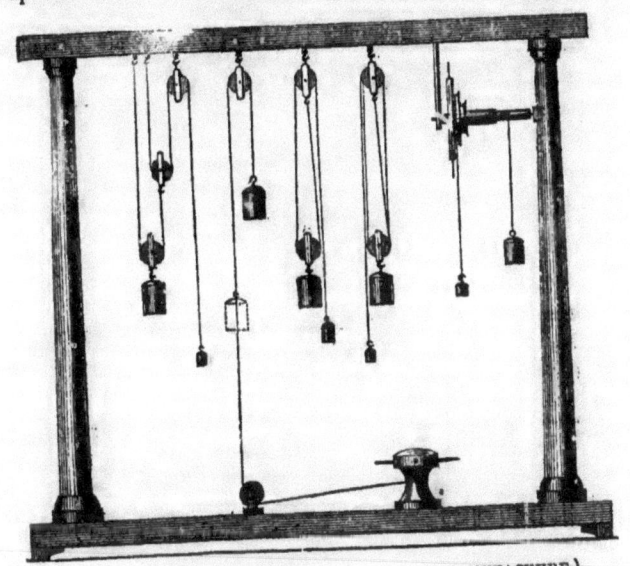

SET OF MECHANICAL POWERS—(CANADIAN MANUFACTURE.)

COMPOUND LEVERS AND WEDGE.

longer, can perform the work of many men acting at once, whom it might be impossible from various causes to bring together at one time. To illustrate this a printer, by means of a screw, can press a sheet of paper against the type, so as to take of a clear impression ; to do which without the aid of the press, the pressure of men would scarcely be sufficient, besides fortynine out of the fifty men would be idle, except just at the instant of pressing. Hence the screw may be said to do the work of fifty men.

40 Johnson's Philosophical Diagrams.—Natural Philosophy.
Rotary Map-stand.—This stand contains six maps or a continuous web of cloth same as engraving No. 1, page 9. Natural Philosophy Map-case same as engraving No. 6, page 11.

List of Plates.

I. Properties of Bodies, containing 37 Diagrams.

II. Mechanical Powers, containing 47 Diagrams.

III. Hydrostatics, containing 28 Diagrams.

IV. Hydraulics, containing 36 Diagrams.

V. Physiology, plate 1, containing 28 illustrations.

VI. Physiology, plate 2, 42 illustrations completing the subject.

Size of map 4 feet 2 inches by 3 feet 6 inches; size of stand 6 feet 9 inches by 4 feet 8 inches. Price of the six, already published, in the Rotary stand $25. Price singly, with hand-book, $2.38.

---

41. Chambers' Scientific Charts of Natural Philosophy.—I. Laws of Matter. II. Laws of Motion. III. Laws of ——, etc. Price $1 each, as published, on rollers.

COLLISION BALLS,

INERTIA APPARATUS.

42. Mechanical Powers, mahogany frame, with three sets brass pulleys, with silk cord, and balanced, two sets brass weights, simple and compound levers, wheel and axle, screw and lever with nut, screw as an inclined plane, wedged in sections, inclined plane with arc and binding screw carriage, ship's capstan, &c., complete (as above.) Price $16.

43. Collision Balls, mahogany stand, six 1¼ inch balls. Price $3.50.

44. Bent Lever, convertable into a Toggle Joint Press with weights, and description. Price $1.50.

45. Inertia Apparatus, (a card being projected by the spring and leaving the ball upon the pillar.) Price 60 cts.

46. Centre of Gravity Apparatus.—A set of eight illustrations for centre of gravity, viz., 1, 2, 3, blocks of various figures, with centres of gravity, and suspension 4, two balls on rod, with centre of gravity; 5 Leaning Tower of Pisa, with two centres of gravity; 6, loaded wheel on stand, with centre of gravity and magnitude; 7, mechanical paradox—a double cone *appears to roll up hill*; 8, horseman, balanced on two points. This set also includes a brass plumb, cord and handle, for supporting the various articles on centre of gravity. Price of set, $8.75.

47. The Brachystochrone, or line of swiftest descent; six feet in length, made of mahogany, with two ivory balls. The curved path is that of a cycloid, and when two balls are released from the top of the inclined plane and the cycloidial curve at the same time, the latter will reach the bottom first, although the path in which it rolls is the longest. Price $10.

48. Prismatic Cylinder to recompose white light. This is attached to the centrifugal machine, pp. 86, Descriptive Catalogue. Price $1.65.

49. Falling Bodies.—Apparatus for illustrating all the principles of the laws of falling bodies, with a set of apparatus attached to illustrate the theory of the pendulum. Price $30.

50. Centre of Gravity.—Two parallelopipeds of a rhomboidal form, to illustrate centre of gravity. They stand firmly on end when separate, but when placed on one another, they are on the point of falling. Price 25 cts.

51. Oblique Cylinder in two pieces to illustrate the same as preceding. Price 25 cts.

52. Screw.—Apparatus for illustrating the principle of the action of the screw; size of the screw 6 inches long, 3 inches diameter, with square bottomed thread, mounted on a spindle with handle. Price $1.25.

53. Lock.—Large wooden model of a lock, with spring and tumbler, mounted on a blackboard, 15 inches by 10 inches, with an iron key. Price $1.80.

HYDROSTATICS AND HYDRAULICS.

54. Forcing Pump, or fire engine; with stand, cistern, and hose, with lifting pump, glass barrel, cistern and receiving tunnel on the same stand. Price $14.

55. Lifting Pump.—Working model of a common lifting pump, with a glass barrel about 10 inches long and 2 inches diameter; gives a continuous stream of water. Price $1.80.

56. Water Wheels.—Models of water wheels—overshot, breast, and undershot. Price $10.80.

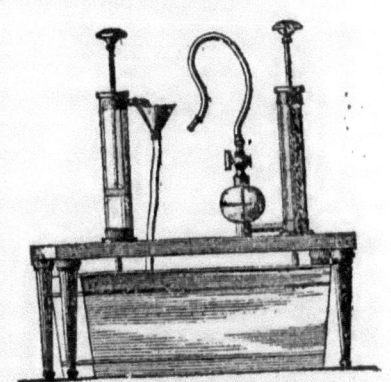

FORCING AND LIFTING PUMP.

C

57. Hiero's Fountain, *of copper,* 12 inches diameter, 40 inches high, with stop cocks, &c. Price $6.50.

58. Hiero's Fountain, *of glass,* by which the operation is seen. Price $8.50 to $12.

59. Archimedes' Screw Pump, with stand and cistern. Price $2.70 to $5.40.

60. Barker's Mill, the moving cistern with four sprays ; mounted on a frame. Price $1.80.

61. Centrifugal Pump, Glass model of the. Price $7.

62. Glass Syphon of the common form. Price 15 cts.

63. Tate's Mercurial Hydraulic Pump, consisting of a bent glass tube with a metal cistern and a wooden plunger. This pump works with about ¼ lb. of mercury put into the end of the tube. It requires no valve. It must be used with a tall glass cylinder kept nearly full of water. In pumping, the downward motion must be slow and the upward quick. Price $1.25.

STEAM.

64. Wightman's Sectional Model of Watt's Low-Pressure Steam Engine and Boiler, with Furnace. Beam 16 inches.......... $38 00

The parts in this model are *truly sectional*—the appearance of one side being an exterior view, while the *reverse* shows the interior, with the piston and valves in motion, as in the real machine.

65. Miniature Steam Engine, High-Pressure, of Brass 13 00

This model is put into motion by a small spirit lamp, and is an interesting illustration of the action of steam as applied to machinery.

66. Revolving Steam Jet, of Brass, complete in itself; illustrates Hero's Steam Engine 1 70

67. Wollaston's Illustration of Low-Pressure Steam Engine...... 0 09

PNEUMATICS.

68. Air Pump: basement of Mahogany ; two barrels ; plate 8 inches, barrel 7½ by 2 inches ; works by a double lever, with bell glass.. 50 00

69. Double Acting Condenser and Exhauster; barrel 7 inches by 1½ ; the change is effected by simply turning the base half round.. 8 70

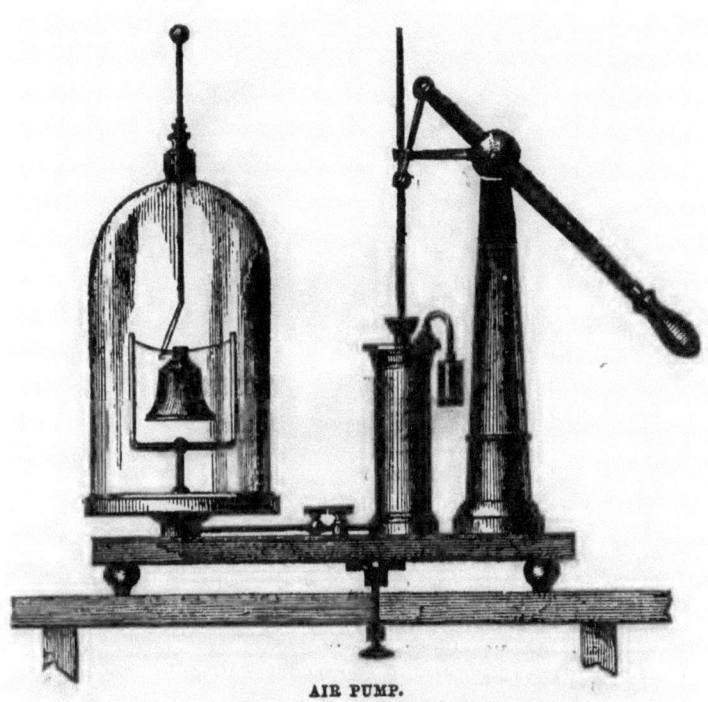

AIR PUMP.

70. Condenser; barrel 7 inches by 1¼; by reversing the piston and Valve, it acts as an Exhauster $5 40

71. Tate's Double Action Air Pump; length of barrel 16 inches, bore 1¼, stroke 8 inches; will freeze water over sulphuric acid under a receiver of 300 cubic inches in 150 strokes; it is mounted on a massive brass clamp with a transfer plate, &c., to convert the apparatus into a condensing pump...................... 18 00

72. Swelled Bell Glasses; 4 sizes; one gallon, $1.50; two gallons $2.40; four gallons $4.20; eight gallons 8 50

73. Swelled open top Bell Glasses, with glass covers; capacities, one gallon $2.40; two gallons $3.60; four gallons.......... 4 80

74. Bell Glasses with screw caps, to receive a stop-cock, &c., (also suitable for collecting gases), six sizes; two quarts $1.80; three quarts $2|40; four quarts $3.00; six quarts $3.60; eight quarts $4.20; twelve quarts.................................... 5 40

75. Hand Glass to show pressure of air for mercury tunnel, &c.... 0 90

76. Stand, Lever and Fulcrum, used with hemispherical cup for weighing a column of air................................. 5 40

77. Freezing Apparatus, bell glass, pan for acid, improved silvered water cup and stand..................................... 4 80

SWELLED BELL GLASS.

78. Revolving Jet, for condensed air fountain $1 20

79. Double revolving Jet, revolves in opposite directions 2 20

80. Bell for vacuo, with stand; the bell is entirely insulated. $1.40 and 2 75

81. Brass Plate and Wood Cylinder; illustrating the porosity of wood, pressure of air, &c............................... 1 10

82. Lock for striking flint and steel in vacuum................ 2 20

83. Barometer in vacuo; bell glass, 33 inches high, tube, cup and cap...................................... 3 60

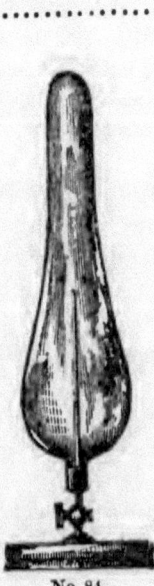
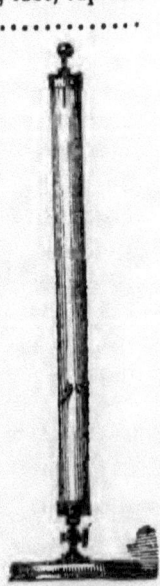

No. 83.   No. 84.   No. 85

84. Artificial Fountain, or fountain in vacuo, with stopcock and jet, stand, &c., 20 inches $4 60
85. Guinea and feather apparatus, with tall conical receiver, sliding rod plate, drop tables, &c; 3 feet, $8.40; 4 feet.... 12 00
86. Guinea and feather apparatus; two falls, ground brass plate and stuffing box; extra hook for use with the Bell, &c.......... 4 50
87. Guinea and feather tube; improved, capped at each end, with stopcock and stand, and made heavy and strong for showing the resistance of condensed air [also fitted for Aurora Tube for Electricity]; 2½ feet, $4.80; 3 feet 7 50
88. Mercury Tunnel for showing the porosity of wood, pressure of air, &c. 0 85

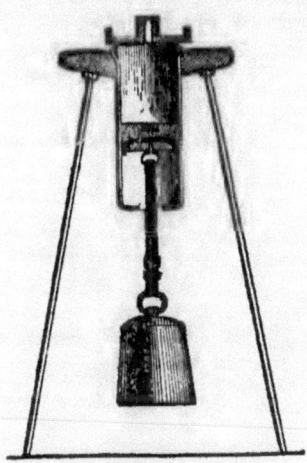

UPWARD PRESSURE APPARATUS.

89, Upward Pressure Apparatus; glass bell; brass cap, with India rubber bag, to which weights are attached; tripod stand and strap... 5 40
90. Bursting Squares; for expansion or pressure, per doz........ 1 80
91. Wire Guard for Bursting Squares......................... 0 60
92. Water Hammer; hermetically sealed, showing that the collision of water in a vacuum produces a sharp noise like solid bodies.. 1 20
93. Sliding Rod; with packing screw, regulating screws, hook and pincers, &c... 1 60
94. Sliding Rod, with Packing Screw......................... 1 20
95. Sheet Rubber Bag, with cap and hook, $1.35; with stop cock 2 20
96. Large Copper Condensing Chamber, globe form, with foot, ten inches in diameter, with stop-cock and interior jet.......... 10 80
97. Pneumatic and Hydrostatic Paradox (for supporting a ball on a jet of air water) includes paradox, tunnel and ball.......... 1 63

98. Plate Paradox, with mica disk, the disk, though lying loose upon the plate, cannot be blown off $1 10
99. Pipe Paradox, with balls............................. 1 10
100. Small Thermometer to suspend in the Flask.............. 0 90
101. Wood Cylinder, and weight for sinking when the air is removed from the pores............................... 0 30
102. Cartesian Bottle Imp, with a glass jar, 12 inches by 3 inches, on foot, with a piece of caoutchouc, 6 inches square, to tie over the mouth of the jar when the imp is put into the water, $3.25, and.............................. 1 10
103. Jar, with foot 15 inches high, 2 inches diameter, with light glass flask to swim in the jar, to illustrate specific gravity... 0 60
104. Bacchus Experiment—a pair of narrow bottles connected by a tube, to show the transfer of liquids from one vessel to another, by the pressure of air under the receiver of Air Pump....... 0 40
105. Bacchus Experiment with brass caps, &c................. 1 80
106. Fire Syringe or Pneumatic Tinder Box, for igniting tinder by compressed air.. 0 90
107. Magic Bottle, from which water will flow through the bottom when the stopper is removed 0 90
108. Perforated Tin Bottle to show the upward pressure of the air 0 60
109. India Rubber Spherical Bags, for expansion; various prices.
109½. Japanned Tin Oiler................................ 0 45
110. Barometer Tube, 31 inches long, with small funnel for performing the Torricellian experiment........................ 0 50
111. Brass Stop-cocks, Connecters, &c.; various prices.

ELECTRICITY.

ELECTRICAL BELLS.   UNIVERSAL DISCHARGER.

112. Electrical Bells; set of three bells with frame to suspend to conductor $3 25
113. Universal Discharger; large insulated table, swelled pillars with universal joints, sliding rod with balls, &c............. 6 50

114. Leyden Jar, improved form, with moveable coatings........ $3 00
115. Electric Spoon for igniting ether.......................... 0 90
116. Dancing Image plates; eleven inches diameter, to suspend to prime conductor.............. 2 20
117. Dancing Image Plates; eleven inches, on adjusting stand............................... 3 30
118. Insulating Stool; mahogany, 8 inch, swelled legs; neatly finished........................ 4 40
119. Insulating Stool; polished wooden top, 13 inches by 11 inches, four massive glass legs.... 1 60
120. Miser's Plate; 12 inches square; plain...... 1 20
121. do do mahogany frame, 1 80
122. Electric Seasons Machine, or Tellurian; mounted on insulated stand..................... 3 30

DANC. FIGURES.

123. Electrical Orrery, for showing the revolution of the moon round the earth, and of the earth and moon around the sun.. 1 25
124. Electrical Inclined Plane............................. 3 60
125. Thunder House, for showing the effects of a stroke of lightning 1 00
156. Electrical Pistol, for exploding the oxyhydrogen gas 1 20
127. Electrical Gas Pistol; plain 0 60
128 ... ...ical Swan and Basin 1 20
129. . ...wan................................... 0 45
130. Ar... ...ider, for attraction and repulsion 0 60
131. Ania ... Box, 30 cts. and 0 60
132. Stout ... of Sealing Wax, 12 inches long................. 0 60
133. Roll of Tin Foil.. 0 20
134. Dutch Gold, per Book................................. 0 10
135. Gutta Percha insulating stands, about 5 inches high, with needle tips..................................... 0 25
136. Gutta Percha insulating stands, about 5 inches high, with flat circular table tops 0 25

WATER BUCKET.   JOINTED DISCHARGER.

137. Water Bucket, to show electrified water $0 60

138. Jointed Discharger, with glass handle (small size)......... $1 25
139. Aurora Borealis Apparatus; consisting of a brass plate with three spikes to screw into the plate of the air pump, and another ground brass plate with three spikes, adapted to the top of the cylinder of the Guinea and Feather apparatus.......... 2 10
140. Head of Hair, for showing electrical repulsion when placed on the conductor of the Machine.......................... 0 75
141. Glass Plume, for the same experiment.............. ..... 0 75

MAGNETISM AND ELECTRO-MAGNETISM.

BOX OF MAGNETIC APPARATUS.

142. Wightman's Improved Box of Magnetic Apparatus........ 6 00
143. U Magnets from 25 cts. to.. .... 1 60
144. Set of two Bar Magnets, with Armatures in a Box; 60 cts. and 0 90
145. Natural Loadstone, or Magnetic Iron Ore; specimen in Box; 30 cts and............................... .... 0 45

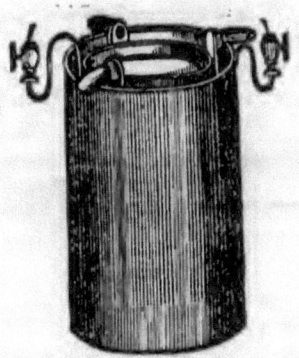

SULPHATE OF COPPER BATTERY.

146. Sulphate of Copper Battery; this Battery is charged with a solution of Sulphate of Copper, (blue vitriol,) by which the power of the Battery is sustained..................... $6 50

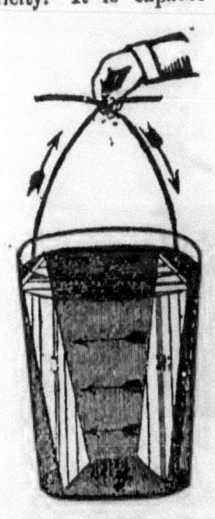

147. Grove's Battery, with Platinum Plates, amalgamated Zinc Cylinders, Porous Cups, and Glass Jars, used with strong Nitric and dilute Sulphuric Acids. 4 series in a Box 8 75
This Battery is the most powerful that has yet been constructed.

148. Smee's Battery; Set of six in a Mahogany Tray, with connectors so arranged as to produce either *quantity* or *intensity* of Electricity. It is capable of evolving, when used with the Water decomposing Apparatus, one cubic inch of the mixed gases in three minutes, and will readily fuse Platinum or Iron wire (used with dilute sulphuric acid).......... 10 80

GROVE'S BATTERY.

149. Daniell's Battery; Set of six pints in a Mahogany tray, capable of decomposing water so as to yield one cubic inch of the mixed gases in three minutes, and will show the deflagration of metals, &c. This Battery is excited by a saturated solution of sulphate of copper in the outer cell, and dilute sulphuric acid iu the inner cell.. 10 80

150. Zinc Plates for Smee's Battery, each 0 35

151. Apparatus for decomposing water, and collecting the gases separately 0 80

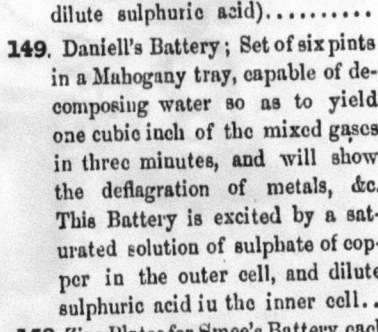

SIMPLE BATTERY.

152. Apparatus for showing the Decomposition of Water, by means of the current from the Magneto-Electric Machine......... $4 20

OERSTED'S ELECTRO, ETC.

153. Oersted's Electro-Magnetic Experiment, for showing deflection of a Magnetic Needle.. 2 00

ELECTRO-MAGNET AND KEEPER.

154. Electro-magnet and Keeper, a single coil; will carry 112lbs 3 00
155. Electro-magnet and Keeper, smaller size................. 1 50

156. Electro-magnetical Coil, with handles $8 20

    This apparatus, when connected with a single cell battery,
is capable of giving powerful shocks, which may be easily
moderated by withdrawing the bundle of wires.

157. Self-acting Electro-Magnetic Apparatus, consisting of Coil,
with Vibrator, Sulphate of Copper Battery, and pair of handles
and Box... 12 00

158. Horizontal Galvanic Machine, for experimental or medical
purposes, with regulator, on mahogany stand 3 50

159. Mariners' Compasses—various prices.

160. Morse's Telegraph, with clock work, reel, alarm, and brake. ⎫
Signal Key for operating do......................... ⎬ 45 00
Paper reel and paper................. ⁝.............. ⎭

161. Large English Telegraph Model, with table of signs, and a 6
inch needle, for use at lectures .... 5 40 and 3 60

162. A Reverser for use with the electric telegraph model, and
other galvanic experiments............................ $5 40

163. Double Beam Axial Engine............................ 20 00

164. Magnetic Toys—ships, fish, swan, &c., in boxes, with magnets,
various prices.

OPTICS.

165. Series of seven lenses and half lenses, each $2\frac{1}{2}$ inches diameter,
in a divided box, lined with velvet 6 60

166. Model, to show the action of the telescope and microscope,
with ground focussing glass, mounted in sliding brass tubes.. 2 10

167. Set of seven mirrors mounted to reunite the seven prismatic
colors, and recompose white light........................ 11 50

168. Camera Obscura....................................... 2 25

MICROSCOPES.

169. The Student's Model Microscope consists of a compound
body, with rack adjustment, on firm tripod stand, with dia-
phram, mirrors, condensing lens, two Huyghenian eye-pieces,
A and B, and two achromatic object glasses. No. 1 Object
glass is of large aperture, $1\frac{1}{2}$ inch focus, magnifying 30 diameters with the A eye-piece, or 900 times superficial. No. 2
Object glass is a triplet of $\frac{1}{4}$ inch focus, magnifying 150
diameters, with the A eye-piece, and 200 diameters with the
B eye-piece, or 40,000 times superficial. Each Microscope is

furnished with printed directions for use, a few thin glass covers, and two glass slides; and is neatly packed in an upright polished mahogany cabinet with lock and key. No. 25. $15 00

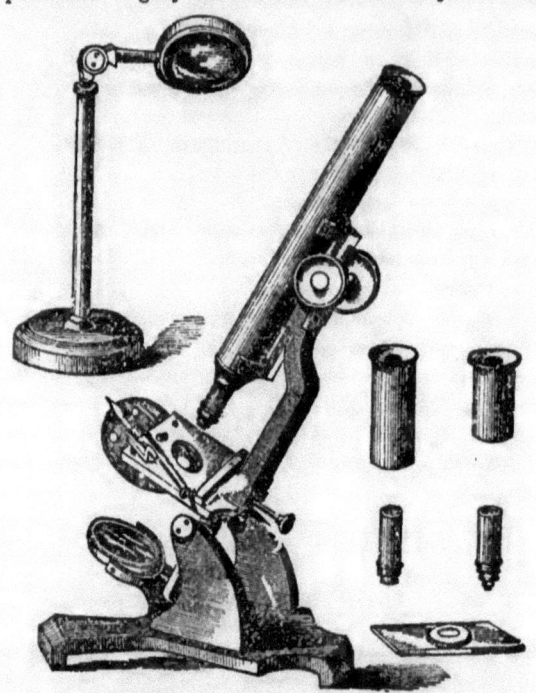

170. Compound School Microscope, on firm tripod stand; with mirror, two object glasses, tweezers, and six objects in upright polished cabinet with drawer. No. 21..................... 3 00

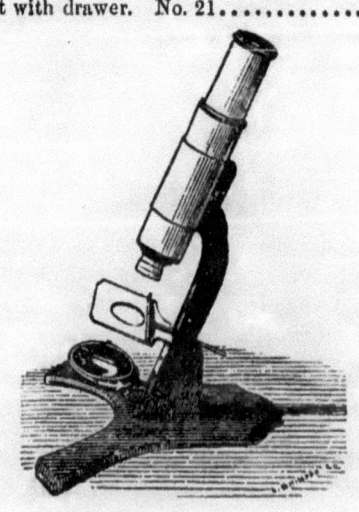

171. Simple Microscope, with rack movement, mirror, three powers, tweezers, glass slides, and two objects, in mahogany case, $3 50

172. Microscope Preparations, Class A; an introductory set, consisting of 24 preparations of various kinds, neatly fitted in a leather case, accompanied by a descriptive Essay, entitled, "Microscopic Revelations."..............................   2 20

173. Best Preparations, mounted in balsam or fluid, including recent and fossil infusoria; spicules of sponges, and gorgonias; blood discs; insect dissections; parasites; vegetable preparations, viz., mosses, algae, fungi, wood sections, spiral and other vessels, cuticles, petals, &c.; case containing two dozen objects,   4 00

174. Neatly Mounted Objects, for beginners, on slides, (assorted insect, vegetable, and other preparations.)   Per case of 24 objects 0 60

175. Griffin's Microscopic Objects; per box 2 00

MAGIC LANTERNS.

176. Magic Lantern, with Lamp and Reflector, giving a clear and defined picture 6 feet in diameter 3 25

177. Magic Lantern, with Argand Lamp and Reflector of superior construction, affording a bright and well illuminated picture from 8 to 10 feet in diameter.............................   6 25

PHANTASMAGORIA LANTERNS.

The Phantasmagoria Lantern gives pictures of greater brilliancy and distinctness than those given by the Magic Lantern. It is used in the same way—the picture being thrown upon a white cloth or a white-washed wall, or upon a transparent screen consisting of wet calico suspended evenly between the Lantern and spectators.

178. No. 1 Phantasmagoria Lantern					$1 00
179. " 2	do	do			1 40
180. " 3	do	do	with superior lamp, 2 in. lens.		2 75
181. " 4	do	do	do	2½ in. lens	3 75
182. " 5 Best	do	do	do	2½ in. lens	5 50
183. " 6	do	and best lamp,		3½ in. lens	8 00
184. " 7	do	do		3½ in.	

achromatic lenses.....................................$11 to 15 00

185. " 8. Griffin's Phantasmagoria Lantern; with 3¼ inch condensers and rack—work adjustment to the lenses; opening for sliders 4¼ inches; gives a disc 10 feet in diameter; in a box.. 16 50

SLIDES.

186. Slides for No. 1	per doz.	75 cts.	to 1 00
187. Slides for No. 2	do	$1 60	to 2 40
188. Slides for No. 3	do	3 00	to 5 00
189. Slides for No. 4	do	4 20	to 9 00
190. Slides for No. 5, framed	do	7 80	to 12 00
191. Slides for No. 6	do	12 00	to 18 00

Astronomical Diagrams on Sliders, for showing the position, size, and principal phenomena of the Solar System,—adapted for use in Public Schools and Mechanics' Institutes, rendering the Science of Astronomy easily comprehensible.

192. No. 1, Set of 12 slides....................................	3 60
193. " 2, do do	4 80
194. " 3, Set of 13 slides, three of them moveable	8 50
195. " 4, a Set of the same character, but better finished	15 75

Picturesque Views, in sets specially arranged for *Dissolving* Views, painted in the first style.

196. The Seasons, an exhibition of Meteorological Phenomena; Rainbow, Aurora Borealis, Snow-fall, Storm, &c.; 10 subjects 18 00

197. Mount Vesuvius, View by Day and Night; an Eruption, with rackwork, showing Smoke, Fire, &c., in motion; 4 subjects... 10 20

198. Picturesque Views, Phenomena of Nature, Illustrations of the War with Russia, &c., &c....................from $1 20 to $2 each.

199. Chromatropes, or Artificial Fire Works .... from 2 00

NATURAL HISTORY.

200. No. 1, Zoology: 36 Figures of Beasts, Birds, Insects, &c., on 12 slides.. $3 60

201. No. 2, Zoology: 48 Figures of ditto, on 12 slides......... 5 40

202. No. 3, do do for large Lanterns.......... 13 60

203. Microscope for Phantasmagoria Lantern, with a set of three slides.. 14 50

204. Cloth for a screen for the Magic Lantern, (when wet it may be hung between the lantern and the audience as a transparent screen,) 9 feet by 10¼ feet, without a seam................ 3 75

HEAT.

205. Pyrometer; this consists of an iron bar and plate gauge, to show that metals expand in all directions when heated.. .... 1 20

206. Model Thermometer, to illustrate the expansion of liquids by heat; 16 ounce flask, with 36 inch tube, scale printed on white wood, 30 inches long, comprehending 100°, from 60° to 100° Fahrenheit. The apparatus is to be filled at 60°, up to the mark 60°, with water colored blue by sulphate of indigo, and is then to be heated over a lamp...................... 1 00

207. Pair Planished Reflectors; 13 inch, in cases which serve for stands, iron ball and stand 8 10

208. Brass Reflectors, true parabolic, on stands, with iron ball, new and convenient arrangement for adjusting the foci, per pair 10 80

209. Concave Reflectors, silvered copper, burnished, 6 inches diameter, with rod, foot, and thumb screws................ 1 50

210. Pulse Glass, consisting of a tube with two bulbs, large size, for showing the ebulition of spirits in vacuo, on applying the heat of the hand; mounted on a stained wooden support 1 25

211. Conductometer for showing the capacity of different metals to conduct heat by the firing of phosphorus, from $1.10 to.. 2 20

Thermometers manufactured by Potter, Toronto, for Public Schools, under the direction of the Educational Department:

212. 8 in. Lancewood Thermometer 0 38

213. 8 in. Boxwood Thermometer, double scales, from 85 cts. to.. 0 95

214. 10 in. do do do do $1 00 to.. 1 15

215. 12 in. do do do do 1 15 to.. 1 30

216. *9 in. Minimum Thermometer......................... 2 00

---

* This is a self-registering Thermometer, and gives two indications, viz., the actual temperature at the time of observation, and the lowest temperature that has occurred since the index was set.

CHEMISTRY.

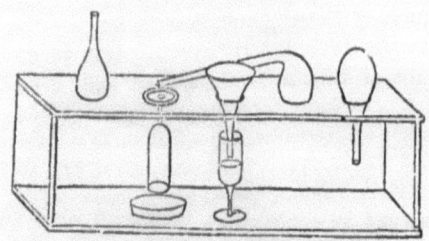

217. Hydrogen Balloons, of gold beaters skin, from............ $1 00
218. Pneumatic Cisterns of copper and tin, various prices.
219. Plain and Tubulated Retorts, from a gill to two quarts, from 40 cts. to 1 50
220. Hydrogen Gas Generator; with gas jet, &c 4 80
221. Superior Gas Bags, India Rubber cloth, with brass connector, from 2 00
222. Small Copper Canister, Screw and Hose, for making Hydrogen, very useful for charging Compound Blowpipes and filling Balloons 2 40
223. Brass Hydrogen Bubble Pipe 0 90
224. Alcohol Blast Lamp, of Copper ; useful in bending Glass Tubes, heating Platina Crucibles, and other purposes where an intense heat is required 2 50
225. Pyrometer, simple and sensitive, with Spirit Lamp........ 4 40
226. Glass Blower's Lamp, Danger's pattern 1 10
227. Blowpipe Apparatus, in a box......................... 5 00
228. Funnel holders, with moveable arm .... from.. 0 30
229. Vertical support and retort holder, with rod, loaded foot & nut 1 00

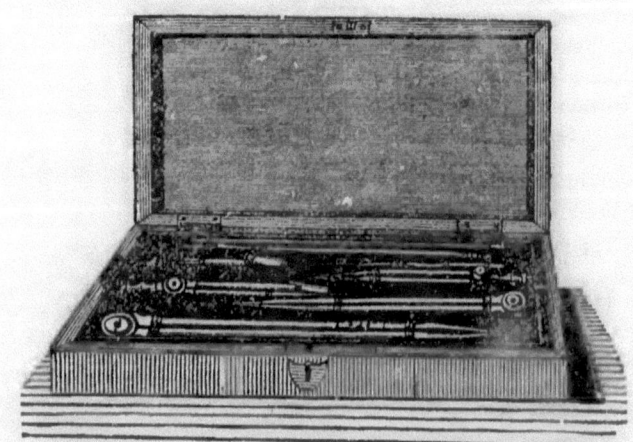

MAHOGANY CASE OF DRAWING INSTRUMENTS.—(SEE NEXT PAGE.)

DRAWING AND MATHEMATICAL INSTRUMENTS.

Department of Science and Art Mathematical Instruments.

230. Mahogany lock case, with tray, containing brass 6 inch steel joint compass, pen and pencil points, divider, bow pen, bow pencil, hand pen, pencil, ivory protractor, scale, and ebony parallel, (0132) $3 60

231. 5 inch covered cardboard case, containing brass compass, pencil point, pen point, and patent scale, (0214) 0 40

232. Cronmire's Case of Mathematical Instruments, containing 12 inch Rule, set square, pair of 6 inch compasses, pen and pencil legs 0 75

233. Do containing pair of 6 inch compasses, pen and pencil legs, bow pen and pencil, ruling pen and scale.................. 1 75

234. Kentish's Treatise on a Box of Instruments, and the side rule for the use of students, engineers, &c., by Thos. Kentish, Am. Edi. hcb.. 0 80

235. Negretti and Zambra's Drawing Instruments: A set of Drawing Instruments, (No. 874,) consisting of one pair of 5 inch sector-jointed, steel-pointed compasses, with fine points; one pair of 6 inch sector-jointed, steel-pointed compasses, with hair points and moveable leg, with pen and pencil holder to fit; bow pencil holder; bow pen, with double joint and spring; ruling pen in ebony handle; turnscrew; pencil; ebony parallel rule, with brass fittings; an ivory protractor, divided to degrees, having on it ten scales of equal parts, a diagonal scale, a line of chords, and sector, 6 inch long, fully divided; in mahogany case.. 12 00

236. Ditto: A set of Drawing Instruments, (No. 875,) consisting of a pair of 3¼ inch steel-pointed, brass-jointed compasses, with one moveable leg; jointed pen and pencil holder to match; a pair of 4½ inch, steel-pointed, brass-jointed compasses; one pair of 6½ inch, brass-jointed, steel-pointed compasses, with moveable leg and jointed pen and pencil holders; horn protractor; lengthening bar; turnscrew; ruling pen, with ebony handle and protracting point; and one divided boxwood rule; the whole inclosed in a neat mahogany case 4 25

D

237. Ditto: A set of Drawing Instruments, (No. 876,) consisting of one pair of 4 inch, brass-jointed, steel-pointed compasses: one pair of 5 inch brass-jointed, steel-pointed compasses, wit. moveable leg: horn protractor; jointed pen and pencil holders; lengthening bar; ruling pen, with ebony handle and protracting point; turnscrew, crayon holder, and divided boxwood scale.. $3 00

238. Ditto: A set of Drawing Instruments, (No. 877,) consisting of a pair of steel-pointed, 6 inch brass-jointed compasses, with one moveable leg; jointed pen and pencil holder, lengthening bar, crayon holder, horn protractor, turnscrew, and divided boxwood scale; in a neat pocket case...................... 3 75

239. Negretti and Zambra's: A set of a Drawing Instruments, (No. 878), consisting of a pair of 5½ inch, steel-pointed, brass-jointed compasses, with one moveable leg; jointed pen and pencil point, crayon-holder, turnscrew, horn protractor, and divided boxwood scale; in a neat pocket case.............. 2 50

ZOOLOGY.

CANADIAN NATURAL HISTORY.

240. Case No. 1.—Working Bees, with section of comb 1 00

241. Case No. 2.—Typical cases of Stuffed Birds, containing specimens characteristic of each of the Orders, and some of the principal Families or genera. Price from $12 to 30 00

242. Case No. 3.—Typical cases containing a single specimen of either of the Orders, Raptores, Insessores, Scansores, Rasores, Grallatores, or Natatores. Price from $1.50 to............. 3 00

243. Case No. 4.—External Anatomy, containing a specimen with printed explanations of all those parts which are exposed to sight. Price from $1.50 to............................... 3 00

PHYSIOLOGY AND ZOOLOGY.

244. **Johnston's Atlas of Human Anatomy and Physiology:**

Plate	I. The Bones.	Plate	VI. Lymphatics and
	II. Ligaments.		Organs of Digestion.
	III. Muscles.		
	IV. Heart and Arteries.		VII. The Brain and Nerves.
	V. Veins and Organs of Respiration.		VIII. The Senses.

Size of Plate 26 inches by 21, folded. Price with hand-book fully explaining the Plates, bound in cloth, or on rollers (2).. 4 75

245. Day & Son's Extinct Animals.—Six Diagrams of the
Extinct Animals of the Ancient World, prepared by B.
Waterhouse Hawkins, F.G.S., for the English Department of
Science and Art:

No. I. The Great Marine Lizards
of the Lias.
No. II. The Gigantic Terrestrial
Lizard of the Oolite.
No. III. Ditto of the Wealden.
*All belonging to the Secondary
Epoch f the Earth's History.*

No. IV. The Pachydermata of the
Tertiary Period.
No. V. Edentata, or Megatheroid
Mammalia of the Tertiary Period.
No. VI. The Great Elephants and
Carnivora of the Past
Tertiary Period.

Double Tinted Lithography, size 40 by 29¼. Mounted on
Rollers and varnished. Price.......................... $12 00

Christian Knowledge Society's Natural History Object Lessons, Small Type Series:

246. Per set of 162, on sheets colored, with hand book......... 7 25
247.   Do   do   without it.............. 6 50
248. Per set of 162, colored, stretched on frames and varnished.. 28 50
249.   Do   plain, on sheets, with hand book........... 4 75
250.   Do   do   without it 3 50
251. List of Object Lessons, size, including letter press, 11 inches
by 12. The Common and Technical name of each specimen
is given: From 1 to 150, see Descriptive Catalogue, pp. 56-7.

151. Rocky Mountain Flying
Squirrel.
152. The Cuckoo.
153. The Mandrill.
154. The Egyptian Vulture.
155. The Dorcas Gazelle.
156. The Blue and Yellow
Macaw.

157. The Oyster.
158. The Humming Bird.
159. The Long Tailed Tit-
mouse.
160. The Manater.
161. The Egyptian Cobra.
162. The Vampire Bat.

**252. Christian Knowledge Society's Tabular View of
the Orders and Families of Fishes:** Four sheets mounted
on rollers and varnished; size 27 inches by 36 inches. Price   1 50

253. Patterson's Animals; How they are classified by Robert
Patterson, M.R.I.A. 18mo. Cloth, limp. pp. 50. Price...   0 22
This is intended as a Key to Patterson's Diagrams. See
pages 58-60 of the Descriptive Catalogue.

254. Redfield's General View of the Animal Kingdom,
including several hundred figures of the RADIATES, MOLLUSKS,
ARTICULATES, and VERTEBRATES, carefully and beautifully
colored after Nature. Cloth, rollers, and vanished. Size, 4ft.
6in. by ft. 3in., with No. 255 ....   8 00

255. **Redfield's Zoological Science; or, Nature in Living Forms.** Illustrated by numerous plates, adapted to elucidate the Chart of the Animal Kingdom. By A. M. Redfield. 12mo, cloth, pp. 700. Price of Chart and Book...... $8 00

BOTANY.

256. **Day & Sons Botanical Diagrams.** Prepared for the Department of Science and Art, by the Rev. Prof. Henslow, &c. Drawn from Nature and on Zinc, by Mr. W. Fitch. Nine Diagrams, size 40¼ by 29, fully colored, mounted and varnished. Price for the set 18 00
   On each side of the Diagrams a Key to the Illustrations, the Classifications, and important characters is given.
257. Christian Knowledge Tabular View of the Vegetable Kingdom, arranged according to the Natural Orders. Four sheets, mounted on rollers, and varnished, size 27 inches by 36 inches. Price 1 50
258. Christian Knowledge Botanical Diagrams, set of 26, with Notes on Elementary Lectures; size 21 inches by 15 inches. Price in sheets, colored.................................... 1 75
   Price colored and mounted on stretchers.................... 7 00

LIST OF TEXT-BOOKS FOR GRAMMAR SCHOOLS IN UPPER CANADA.

Prescribed by the Council of Public Instruction, under the authority of the 6th Section of the Grammar School Act, 15 Vic. ch. 186.

[NOTE.—The Grammar School Trustees can select such text-books from the following list as they may approve; but in no case should more than one series of books be permitted to be used in each school.]

1. LATIN.

Arnold's First and Second Book, Am. Edi., *dac*	$0 64
First Book, Eng. Edi., *riv*....................................	0 64
Key to ditto	0 22
Second Book, Eng. Edi., *riv*.................................	0 85
Key to ditto...	0 42
Third Book, "Latin word Building," Eng. Edi., *riv*.............	0 96
[Arnold's Verse Composition, 8vo., Eng. Edi., *riv*	1 18
Key to ditto...	0 43
Arnold's First Verse Book, Part I., 12mo., Eng. Edi. *riv*.......	0 43
Ditto, Part II. 12mo., Eng. Edi., *riv*...........	0 22
Andrew and Stoddart's Latin Grammar........................	0 95

Arnold's Prose Composition, 12mo., Am. Edi., *dac*.............. $0 86
   Ditto,   Part I., Eng. Edi., 8vo., *riv*............. 1 40
   Key to ditto 0 38
   Ditto,   Part II., Eng. Edi., *riv*................. 1 70
   Key to ditto 0 32
Anthon's Latin and English Dictionary. 12mo., Am. Edi., *hb*..... 1 72
Bullions' Adam's Grammar, Am. Edi., *fbc*..................... 0 70
Edinburgh Academy Rudiments, *ob* 0 43
Eton Grammar, *lc*. White's, Yonge's, &c.................... . 0 64
   Kaltschmidt's Latin and English Dictionary, 12mo. (Chambers' Educational Course.) $1.92 each, bound together; $1.05 each, Latin part; 95 cts. each, English part.

---

2. GREEK.

Arnold's First Book,* Am. Edi., *dac*.......................... 0 65
   First Book, Eng. Edi., *riv*.............................. 1 05
   Key to ditto 0 32
Second Book, Eng. Edi., *riv*.............................. 1 17
   Key to ditto 0 43
Third Book, Eng. Edi., *riv*.............................. 0 73
Fourth Book, Eng. Edi.................................... 0 85
Arnold's First Prose Composition, Am. Edi., *dac*............... 0 65
Arnold's First ditto, Eng. Edi............................. 1 18
   Key to ditto... 0 80
Arnold's Second Prose Composition, Am. Edi., *dac*........... 0 65
Arnold's Second ditto, Eng. Edi............................ 1 40
   Key to ditto... 0 73
Arnold's Reading Book, Am. Edi., *dac*...................... 1 06
Bullions' Grammar, Am. Edi., *fbc*.......................... 0 86
Edinburgh Academy Rudiments, Eng. Edi., *ob*.......... ...... 0 73
Eton Grammar, Homer's, Routledge's, etc.................... 0 96
Anthon's Prosody, Eng. Edi., 55 cts. each, Am. Edi............. 0 65
Liddell and Scott's Greek Lexicon, (Abridged.) Eng. Edi........ 2 16
Donnegan's Greek Lexicon. 8vo. $3.35 cloth, sheep........... 4 00

CLASSICAL DICTIONARIES, &c.

Smith's Classical Dictionary, illustrated. 8vo. Eng. Edi......... 3 30
Smith's Smaller Classical Dictionary.   ) Illustrated,
Smith's Smaller Dictionary of Antiquities. ∫ 12mo., Eng. Edi.... 1 65

---

* The first and second books are not required to be used in the Grammar Schools, but they are inserted here in order to give the series complete. The sixth book is designed for girls.

Rich's Companion to Latin Dictionary and Greek Lexicon $4 00
Baird's Classical Manual, Am Edi., *bl* 0 43

---

3. FRENCH.

Merlet's Grammar, Eng. Edi., *twm* 1 20
  Grammar: Also, in parts as follows :
    Pronunciation and Accidence 0 80
    Syntax 0 80
    Key to Grammar 0 80
Merlet's Le Traducteur. Eng. Edi. 1 20
Le Traducteur:
    Synonyms explained 0 65
    Stories from French Writers 0 45
    Synopsis of the Language 0 65
    Table of Verbs on a Card 0 14
Merlet's Dictionary of Difficulties. Eng. Edi 1 45
Arnold's First Book, Eng. Edi 1 15
Key to the Exercises 0 53
Arnold's Hand Book of Vocabulary, Eng. Edi 0 96
Noël and Chapsal's Grammar, (in French,) 0 70
  (in English.) 0 65
Collot's Levizac's Grammar . . . . . . ⎫
Collot's Pronouncing Reader . . . . . ⎪
Collot's Interlinear Reader . . . . ⎬ Am. Edi., *'hz* 0 48
Collot's Anecdotes and Questions, . ⎪
Collot's Dialogues and Phrases . . . . ⎭
Key to Collot's Exercises in Grammar 0 32
Collot's French and English Dictionary. 8vo . Am. Edi 3 25
Surrenne's New Manual, Am. Edi., *dac* 0 55
Ditto, Eng. Edi 0 75
Spiers and Surrenne's French and English Dictionary, 12mo., Am.
  Edi., $1 30 ; 8vo. 2 70
Ditto, Eng. Edi 2 25

---

4. ENGLISH.

Lennie's Grammar, *ob* 0 32
Key to ditto 0 75
Bullions' Grammar 0 48
National Grammar 0 08
Sullivan's Grammar 0 18
Art of Reading. (National Series) 0 15
Sullivan's Dictionary of Derivations 0 45

Sullivan's English Dictionary............................ $0 60

The National Readers. Dublin Editions. Price as follows:

First Book 0 02
Second.................... .... 0 07
Third 0 16
Fourth 0 18
Supplement to ditto 0 22
Fifth Book..................................... 0 22
Sixth Book 0 22
Sullivan's Spelling Book Superseded............ 0 22
Sullivan's Literary Class Book 0 50
Whately's Lessons on Reasoning, Eng. Edi., *jwp* 0 37

Whately's Lessons on Christian Evidences, or the Truth of Christianity. (Appendix to 4th National Reader,) Eng. Edi., 8 cts. each, Questions 5 cts. Am. Edi. 22 cts. each, including Questions in a separate pamphlet.

Whately's Introductory Lessons on the British Constitution...... 0 12
Political Economy in Chambers' Educational Course............ 0 43
Spalding's English Literature. Eng. or Am. Edi. *ob. dac.*....... 0 70
Reid's Rudiments of English Composition, Eng. Edi. *ob*......... 0 40
Key to ditto 0 70

---

5. MATHEMATICS.

Arithmetic in Theory and Practice. (National Series) Eng. Edi... 0 25
Key to ditto 0 27
Thompson's, (James, LL.D., Glasgow) Arithmetic 0 68
Key to ditto................................... 1 33
Thompson's, (James, LL.D., Glasgow) Algebra.................. 0 96
Loomis' Treatise on Algebra 0 85
Colenso's Simpson's Euclid.................................... 1 12
Colenso's Algebra, Part I 0 85
Key to ditto 1 23
Potts' Euclid... 0 75
Mensuration 0 14
Appendix to ditto.... .... 0 12
For Mathematical Instruments, see page 40.

---

6. GEOGRAPHY AND HISTORY.

Sullivan's Introduction to Geography and History.............. 0 13
Sullivan's Geography Generalised............................. 0 45
Epitome of Geographical Knowledge (National Series).......... 0 27
Hodgins' Geography and History of Canada and of the other
British Colonies 0 50

White's Elements of General History, Parts I. II. III., (Ancient,
Middle Ages, and Modern) bound together, $1.30. In parts .. $0 70
White's History of Great Britain and Ireland, Eng. Edi., *ob*...... 0 70
White's History of France 0 70
Schmitz's Manual of Ancient History. Part I. 0 90
   Do.   do.   do.   Part II................. 0 90
Putz's Ancient Geography and History. By Arnold & Paul 0 85
Putz's Mediæval Geography and History. Do. Am. Edi., *duc*.... 0 65
Putz's Modern Geography and History. Ditto.................. 0 85
Johnston's General School Atlas ....⎫
Johnston's Physical School Atlas ....⎬ 2 50
Johnston's Classical School Atlas ....⎭
Pillans' Physical and Classical Geography, (Companion to Johnston's Classical Atlas)..................................... 0 80

7. PHYSICAL SCIENCE.

Third National Book, Dub. Edi............................... 0 18
Fourth National Book, Dub. Edi.............................. 0 22
Fifth National Book, Dub. Edi............................... 0 32
Youman's Chemical Atlas, with thirteen coloured plates. pp. 105.
  Am. Edi. 4to... 1 70
Youman's Chemistry, with coloured Chart 5 00
  Ditto, without Chart 0 63
Olmsted's School Philosophy................................. 0 80
Johnston's six Charts of Natural Philosophy, with Hand-Books,
  each... 2 38
Patterson's First Steps to Zeology, Parts I. and II., together..... 0 58

8. MISCELLANEOUS.

Hullah's Manual of Vocal Music............................. 1 05
Exercises and Figures contained in the Manual. Parts I. and II.
  each 0 18
Large Sheets, containing the Figures in the Manuals, in parcels,
  as follows: Nos. 1 to 8, 9 to 16, 17 to 24, 25 to 32, 33 to 40.
  Price for each parcel..................................... 1 50
Parcel containing Nos. 41 to 52............................. 2 25
  Do.   do.   do.   stretched on frames and varnished 50 00
School Songs, for two or three voices, composed by Hullah. In
  two books, pp. 16. Each................................. 0 14
Mulhauser's Writing Manual 0 54
National Copy Lines 0 40
Smith's Copy Slips, each 0 10
National Book-Keeping 0 10
Drawing Books and Materials authorized by the Department of
Science and Art, England; and those in the Descriptive Catalogue of the Educational Depository.

DRAWING BOOKS, MATERIALS AND MODELS,

1. DRAWING BOOKS.

Chapman's American Drawing Book, especially adapted to the use of Schools, Academics, and Home Instruction. The Wood Engravings in these works are most exquisitely finished. They embrace every variety of example, from the simple to the highly finished specimens, of drawing of the Human Figure, antique and modern, Natural Scenery &c. &c. Am. Edi. 4to *jsr.*

The following Branches of the Art are treated separately, viz. :—

1. Primary Instruction and Rudiments of Drawing.
2. Drawing from Nature—material and method.
3. Perspective—Composition—Landscape—Figures, &c.
4. Drawing, as applicable to the Mechanic Arts.
5. Painting in Oil and Water Colours.
6. The Principles of Light and Shade.
7. External Anatomy of the Human Form, and Comparative Anatomy.
8. The various methods of Etching, Engraving, Modelling, &c.

						NET CASH PRICE.
Drawing Book, No. I, Elementary. Quarto. Atlas form. pp. 56.						$0 50
Do do No. II, do do do do pp. 56.						0 50
Do do No. III, Perspective do do do pp. 56.						0 50
Drawing Copy Book No. I, Primary and Elementary. Small quarto, pp. 20, singly						0 13
Do per dozen						1 25
Do No. II, Primary and Elementary. Small pp. 20, singly						0 13
Do per dozen						1 25

Williams' Instructions in Drawing, for the use of Elementary Schools, with numerous illustrative Wood Cuts, and Outline Figures of Models sanctioned by Privy Coun. Com. on Education. Eng. Edi., *jwp.* 8vo. pp. 116 ...... 0 60

2. EXAMPLES OF OUTLINE DRAWING, AS FOLLOWS :

Raffaelle's Scripture Outlines, beautifully engraved on steel. Size, 27 inches by 21. Eng. Edi. *tv.* Per set of 9, in sheets 1 50

Raffaelle's do stretched on frames and varnished 3 50

(The following are Authorised by the English Department of Science and Art.)

Familiar Objects, or white Outline Drawings, on brown ground, 2 sheets 0 07

Ditto ditto Mounted on two cards 0 20

Bishop of St. Asaph's Outlines of Familiar Objects, being black
Outlines on white ground (in paper cover)................... $0 16
Ditto   ditto   Mounted............................ 0 65
Taylor and Walton's Linear Drawing Copies, comprising upwards
of 200 subjects on 24 sheets, mounted on thick pasteboard, in a
portfolio 1 25
Simpson's Elementary Free Hand Drawing Copies, Flat examples,
34 figures on 12 sheets, and one containing Letter Press, mounted
on canvas, without rollers, per set........................ 2 00
Robinson's Manual of Elementary Outline Drawing, to be used with
the Flat Examples, each, 18 cts., per dozen............. .... 2 10

3, EXAMPLES OF COLOUR DRAWING.

*(The following are Authorised by the English Department of Science and
Art.)*

Mabrun's French Lithographed Drawings of Machinery, shaded.
Mounted on canvas and rollers, each....................... 4 50
Simpson's Diagram of Color, shewing the relative surface proportion
in which the primary, secondary and tertiary hues harmonise
with each other. 3 diagrams on one sheet, mounted on canvas,
without rollers. Large size 1 50
Small Ditto   ditto   ditto 0 50
Robinson's Collection of Examples of Colored Ornament, beautifully
and richly tinted, per set of twelve, mounted on stretchers and
varnished 4 50
Redgrave's Manual of Color, with a Catechism, each 20 cts., per dozen 2 80
Brookes' Illustrations of Exercises in Elementary Design for deco-
rating surfaces. Given Forms arranged so as to fill given Geometrical Spaces, Lithographed by female class of the Department, in two sheets 0 30
Sower & Barnes' Chalk Drawings, a Series of white outlines on
black ground. 8 Plates 1 00

4. MISCELLANEOUS DRAWING.

French Models in Plaster of Paris, of the hands and feet. Life
Size. Beautiful models for drawing from nature, assorted, each 0 40
Jullen's Studies; various positions of the hands and feet, *rs.* each,
mounted.. 0 55
Ditto. Studies of Heads, various prices.
Ditto The Human Figure, ditto.
Carl Kopper's Drawing Book of Flowers, in paper cases. Eng.
Edi. *wtc* 0 25
Bolton's Drawing from Objects. 8vo. Eng. Edi. *gs* pp. 130..... 1 50
Dibdin's Practical Drawing Book, 24 plates. Plain oblong, 4to .. 1 00
Do . Progressive   do   24 in outline and colours. 48
Plates, oblong, 4to..................................... 2 25

Tegg's Elementary Drawing Book of Landscape, heads, hands, feet, etc $1 10

Chambers' Drawing Books :—Consisting of a Series of Progressive Lessons in Drawing and Perspective, with General Instructions, in Eighteen Books. Oblong 8vo. Per set.................. 6 00

Chambers' Practical Diagrams and Working Drawings for Schools. Edited by Robert Scott Burn, viz:

1. The Styles of Gothic Architecture; comprising Examples of Windows, Buttresses, Crosses, Perforated Parapets, &c., in Norman, Decorated, Geometrical, Curvilineal, Elizabethan, and other styles... 0 25

2. The Orders of Roman Architecture ; comprising Examples of Tuscan, Doric, Ionic, Corinthian, and Composite Columns. The heights and projections of each member carefully marked. Examples of Pedestals, Ballusters, &c...................... 0 25

3. Condensing Beam Steam Engine, in Section, End-elevation and Plan. The dimensions of each part carefully calculated and drawn to scale. Size of each Sheet, 25 by 20 inches, with descriptive reference. On a sheet, 25 cts., mounted 0 50

4. Examples of Ornamental Drawing; being suggestions for Manufacturing and Decorative Designs. In sheets, each......... 0 06

5. Working Drawings and Designs of Steam Engines. Plates and Letter Press. Example No. I. Horizontal High-pressure Engine.. 0 25

6. Illustrations of Machine and Mill Gearing. Plates and Descriptive Letter-press. The subjects illustrated are—Couplings for Shafts, Brackets, Driving Pulleys, Toothed Gearing, Wheel and Pinion, Racks, Crank, Connecting-rods, &c. &c., in Plan, Elevation and Section, drawn to scale 0 25

5. DRAWING MATERIALS.

Parker's Box of Drawing Materials, containing Chalk-holder, Leather and Paper Stumps, Prepared Charcoal, Chamois Leather, and six Crayons, per box......................... 0 63

Ditto best French Crayons, black and white, per box 0 16

Reeves & Sons Box of Drawing Materials, in mahogany box ... 0 70

Ditto   Academy Chalks, black, white, and red, in mahogany box 0 13

Reeves & Sons Carbon..................................... 0 40

Ditto   Brass Porte-Crayon, each 8 cts. Per dozen.......... 0 90

Ditto   Sketch Book. Imperial 4to. Various colors 0 63

Ide & Dutton's Colored Chalk Crayons for blackboards, in box of 12 dozen.............:........................... 1 63

Do   do   do   do   white........... 0 55

Groombridge's substitute for a blackboard. No.1 size, 24 in. by 36   1 50

Do   do   do   No. 2 " 30 " by 36   1 88

Do   do   do   No. 3 " 30 " by 42   2 10

Department of Science and Art, Drawing Materials, in a box ... $0 63
Ditto   Porte-Crayons, each 6 cts. Per dozen 0 60
Ditto   14-inch Compasses for blackboard 0 80
Ditto   Slip, Two Set Squares. and T Square. Per set....... 1 50
Ditto   Black Canvas strained on frame, 22 inches by 17...... 0 50
Negretti and Zambra's Pantagraphs in wood, for copying and reducing plans, drawings, or maps in any required proportion, 15 inches long... 8 25

WRITING.

Mulhauser's Manual of Writing, with 40 model Plates 0 54
Writing Model, first or elementary set, 20 Plates, mounted on card board................... .... 0 54
Ditto   second set; Medium, or half text hand, and the Cyphers 0 22
Ditto   third set; fine. or small hand, and for Punctuation, Proverbs, and Moral Science........ .... 0 22
Ditto   fourth set; fine, or small hand, and the cyphers. List of the Sovereigns of England since the Conquest...... 0 22
Writing Books, ruled for Mulhauser's System, Nos. I, II, and III. No. I ruled with diagonal lines throughout; No. II, the same ruling, alternated with leaves of cross lines only; No. III, ruled for half text. Per dozen 0 65
Ditto   each... .... 0 07
Slates ruled for the Method.................................. 0 16
National Copy Lines, per set of six assorted sheets............. 0 40
Fulton's School Writing Books. Per set of four numbers....... 0 50
Ditto,   per dozen 1 25
No. 1. Designed for Young Beginners. No. 2, Designed to be used after No. 1. No. 3. Designed for Advanced Pupils. No. 4. Contains only the Parallel Lines.
Badlam's Writing Books. The Common School Writing Book. In five numbers. Per set.................................. 0 63
Ditto,   Per dozen.................................... 1 25
Gould's Progressive Penmanship, Practical and ornamental, for the use of Schools, in Five Writing Books, per set........... 0 63
Ditto,   Per dozen................................ 1 25
Writing—Plain, and Current Hand. In ten prepared Copy Books, Foolscap size. Price each...................... .... 0 06
Maclaurin's & Rightmeyer's Writing Books. Per dozen, small size.. 1 25
Christian Knowledge Society's Script Alphabets, two sheets 0 07
Ditto,   Numeral Letters, two sheets 0 06
Darton's Sign Painters' Assistant........................... 0 25
Smith's Copy Slips, *etc.* (oblong 12mo.) contains :—

1. First Writing Lessons.	3. Small Text.
2. Large Text.	4. Round Hand.

5. Small hand.
6. Large Text.   Round style of writing.
7. Small Text, ditto.
8. Round Hand, ditto.
9. Geographical running hand.
10. Commercial ditto.
11. Receipts, Bills of Exchange, &c.
12. Select Sentence.s
13. Ladies' Geographical.

14. Ladies' running hand. Part I
15. Do.   do   Part 2.
16. Do.   do   Part 3.
17. Scripture round hand.
18. Do   do
19. Old English.
20. German Text.
21. Engrossing.
22. Latin Copies.
23. School Ornamental Alphabets.

The foregoing per dozen.................................. $1 13

Singly 0 10

24. A set of Plain and Ornamental Alphabets containing 11 various
    Hands 0 30

25. The Ladies Writing Exemplar, (Edited by D. H. Edwin,) with
    part 3, Ladies' Running Hand Copies 0 25

26. Astronomical Copies, (Edited by R. Mitchell,) engraved by W.
    Smith.. 0 10

Nos. 1 to 23 and 26, assorted, per dozen................. 1 13

MAPS, CHARTS, AND DIAGRAMS OF PHYSICAL GEOGRAPHY.

1. MURAL MAPS, BY PROF. ARNOLD GUYOT.*

Map of the World.. 7 50
 "   North America...................................... 6 50
 "   South America 6 50
 "   Geographical Elements 6 50

Other Maps of the Series are in preparation.

2. PHYSICAL GEOGRAPHY.

Varty's Physical Map of the World, showing its various features
    and phenomena.   Size, 5 ft. 6 in. by 4 ft. 9 in.............. 6 00

Ditto,   Physical Map of Europe, exhibiting its physical features.
    Size, 5 ft. by 4 ft. 4 in................................. 3 75

Ditto,   Physical Map of Palestine 1 00

Johnston's Physical Chart of the World.   Size, 4 ft. 2 in. by 3 ft.
    6 in.. 2 28

Ditto,   Illustrations of Geographical Terms.   Size, 2 ft. 9 in.
    by 2 ft. 3 in... 1 50

Smith's Principal Mountains of the World   Size, 24 in. by 28 in.;
    coloured, mounted and varnished........................ 1 50

---

* This is a series of colored Maps, projected on a large scale, for the Recitation
Room, consisting of a Map of the World, North and South America, exhibiting the
physical phenomena of the Globe, &c.

Smith's Principal Rivers of the World. Size, 24 in. by 28 in.; coloured, mounted and varnished...................... ..... $1 50

Christian Knowledge Society's comparative view of the Principal Rivers in the World. Coloured, mounted and varnished.. 1 50

Ditto, Six sheets of Physical Geography, viz.:—1. Comparative Magnitude of the Principal Countries in the World; and 2. of the Principal Oceans, Seas, Islands, &c. 3. Comparative Heights of the Principal Mountains. 4, Ditto, Length of the Principal Rivers. 5. Ditto, Sizes of the Principal Lakes. 6. Mode of Constructing Maps, &c. Size, 44 in. by 45 in. Colored, mounted and varnished.................. .... 1 50

Ditto, Two Sheets—1. Showing the Isothermal Map of the World. 2. Illustrating the Influence of Climate on Vegetation. Size, 22 in. by 30 in. Coloured, mounted and varnished..... 0 50

Reynolds' Chart of Physical Geography; exhibiting on separate sheets—1. Physical features of the Land. 2. Volcanic system of the Globe. 3. Phenomena and movements of the Waters. 4, Diagram of Climates. 5. Distribution of Winds. 6. Distribution of Rain. Size, about five feet square. On cloth, rollers and varnished.................................. ...... 3 75

Ditto, Twelve Diagrams of Physical Geography—1. Geographical Diagram, moveable, showing the rotation of the Earth, &c. 2. Physical Map of the World. 3. Mountains and Volcanoes. 4. Rivers and Lakes. 5. Waterfalls. 6. Wind and Rain Maps. 7. Tidal Chart of the World, and Botanical Map of the Distribution of Plants. 8. Distribution of Animals, Birds, and Reptiles. 9. Distribution of the Human Race, &c. 10. Varieties of Mankind, &c. 11. Physical Map of the British Isles. 12. The principal Buildings in the World. The Series of Twelve, enclosed in a cloth portfolio.............. 2 70

Ditto, View of Nature—1. In all climates. 2. In sections of the Earth's crust. Two sheets, size 22 inches by 68 inches, colored and varnished, mounted together..... .... 2 70

Ditto, View of Nature, folded; paper portfolio............ 1 05

Ditto, " " cloth, lettered............. 1 85

Ditto, View of Nature, in ascending regions. Colored; size 22 in. by 24 in., mounted and varnished.............. .. .... 1 50

Ditto, in a paper portfolio................................ 1 05

Ditto, cloth and lettered 1 85

GEOLOGICAL MAPS, DIAGRAMS AND CABINETS.

1. MAPS, ATLASES, AND DIAGRAMS.

Smith's Geological Map of the British Isles. Size, 5 ft. 8 in. by 4 ft. 4 in.. 3 75

Marcou's Map—A Geological Map of the United States and British Provinces of North America ; with an explanatory text, geological sections, and Plates of the Fossils which characterize the Formations. By Jules Marcou, 2 vols. 8vo., cloth.............. $3 00

The Map is coloured, and done up with linen cloth back, and folded in octavo form, with thick cloth covers.

Brogniart's Map of Geology, or a graphical exposition of the Section of the Earth so far as it is known. By Professor M. Alexandre Brogniart, Paris. Size, 30 in. by 23 in, Eng. Edi. *rgc*- 1 00

Reynold's Geological Chart, showing at one view the Order of Superposition, Mineral Characters, Principal Fossils, Localities, Thickness, and Uses of the various Stratified Rocks; with illustrative Diagrams. By Alfred W. Morant, C.E., F.G.S. On a sheet 3 feet in height by 2 feet in width, colored, on roller, varnished... 1 00

Ditto, folded in book form, with cover 1 30

Reynolds' Popular Pictorial Atlas of Geology, illustrating and describing the Principles of the Science, revised by John Morris, F.G.S., coloured, 8vo., paper, Eng. Edi., *jr*........... 0 43

Reynolds' Section of the Earth's Crust, on a large scale, showing the general arrangement of the Strata, and the relations of various Rocks to each other ; also the position of the Deposits of Coal, and other Minerals ; gold, silver, and other metallic veins, Coloured, with description by John Morris, F.G.S. On cloth, rollers, and varnished. Size, 3 ft. by 2 ft............. 1 10

Ditto, paper portfolio...................................... 0 66

Ditto, Table of British Strata, showing the order of superposition and comparative thickness of the Stratified Rocks of the British Islands. On a large sheet, about 5 feet in length, coloured, 50 cents ; on roller, varnished..................... 1 00

Ditto, Geognostic Profiles, on the plan of Humboldt and Ritter ; showing the Relief of the Continents, or their vertical elevation above the sea level. By John Emslie. Each profile is colored to indicate the climate of the region illustrated. On four sheets, each 3 feet in length, with description, in paper portfolio, $1 30 the series ; on roller, varnished 2 00

Ditto, Twelve Geological Diagrams—1. Popular Geology, 2. The Antediluvian World. 3. Geological Map of the World, according to eminent authorities. 4. Geological Map of England. 5. Geological Map of Scotland. 6. Geological Map of Ireland. 7. Geological Eminences of the British Islands. 8. Natural Phenomena. 9. Volcanoes and Earthquakes. 10, 11, 12. Section of the Earth's Crust. Six feet long by 1 foot broad. The series enclosed in a cloth portfolio....................... 2 70

Christian Knowledge Society's Tabular view of characteristic British Fossils, stratigraphically arranged. Four sheets mounted on roller, coloured and varnished. Size 27 in. by 36 in..... $1 50

Ditto, folded in book form, with cover........................ 1 30

2. GRIFFIN'S GEOLOGICAL CABINETS, &c.

Fragments of Minerals, from 70 to 80 specimens for blow pipe experiments, in a paper box................................ 1 10

Oak-tin Cabinet, with 54 Minerals for Blow-pipe experiments 2 50

Pasteboard Cabinet, with 44 Minerals.......................... 3 50

Do   do   with Rocks and Fossils.................. ... 3 50

Geological Cabinet, containing 100 Rocks, size, 4 square inches, disposed in the order of their natural position, relative to one another 8 00

Mahogany Cabinet, with 100 Minerals.......................... 8 00

Pasteboard Cabinet with 50 specimens of Minerals, 50 Geological specimens, and 15 Models of remarkable Crystals...... :.... 8 00

100 Mineral Specimens, in Mahogany Cabinet, with Drawers 12 00

100 Rocks in Mahogany Cabinet, with Drawers and Catalogue..... 13 00

Mahogany Cabinet, with Drawers, containing 100 Specimens of Minerals selected from various localities 13 00

Mahogany Cabinet, with Drawers, containing 100 Specimens of Rocks and Fossils, carefully selected from different strata........... 13 00

Pasteboard Geological Cabinet, containing 150 Specimens of Rocks, size, 4 square inches, disposed in the order of natural position, relative to one another 14 00

150 Mineral Specimens in Mahogany Cabinet, with Drawers...... 19 00

Box of 120 Models Crystals, 100 Metallic Ores, size, 4 square inches 24 00

Set of 12 Models of Crystals.... .... 1 20

Tennant's Geological Cabinets, each............... $13 50 and 20 00

3. SOPWITH'S GEOLOGICAL MODELS, IN BOOK-FORM CASES.

The Nature of Stratification :—Of Valleys of Denudation ; Succession of Coal Seams in the Newcastle Coal Field ; Strata of adjacent Lead Mine Districts ; the Effects produced by Faults or dislocations; Intersection of Mineral Veins, &c., are shown in a Series of Models, accompanied with a Letter-press description ; by T. Sopwith, F.G.S. Eng. Edi., jten. Sold in cases, bound and lettered to resemble large octavo, quarto, or folio volumes :—

No. 1. Set of Six Models, each presenting nine square inches of surface...................................... 12 00

No. 2. The same, on a larger scale of sixteen square inches of surface.. .... 15 00

No. 3. Twelve Models, six being the same as No. 1, nine square inches of surface...................................... 24 00

No. 4. The same, on enlarged scale, sixteen square inches of surface 30 00